Sheltie.

The little pony with the big heart

Sheltie is the lovable little Shetland pony with a big personality. His best friend and owner is Emma, and together they have lots of exciting adventures.

Share Sheltie and Emma's adventures in

Peter Clover was born and went to school in London. He was a storyboard artist and illustrator before he began to put words to his pictures. He enjoys painting, travelling, cooking and keeping fit, and lives on the coast in Somerset.

Also by Peter Clover in Puffin

The Sheltie Series

Sheltie
The Big Wish

Peter Clover

PUFFIN BOOKS

Special thanks to Ann Ruffell
To Josie

PUFFIN BOOKS

Published by the Penguin Group
Penguin Books Ltd, 80 Strand, London WC2R 0RL, England
Penguin Putnam Inc., 375 Hudson Street, New York, New York 10014, USA
Penguin Books Australia Ltd, 250 Camberwell Road, Camberwell, Victoria 3124, Australia
Penguin Books Canada Ltd, 10 Alcorn Avenue, Toronto, Ontario, Canada M4V 3B2
Penguin Books India (P) Ltd, 11 Community Centre, Panchsheel Park, New Delhi – 110 017, India
Penguin Books (NZ) Ltd, Cnr Rosedale and Airborne Roads, Albany, Auckland, New Zealand
Penguin Books (South Africa) (Pty) Ltd, 24 Sturdee Avenue, Rosebank 2196, South Africa

Penguin Books Ltd, Registered Offices: 80 Strand, London WC2R 0RL, England

www.penguin.com

First published 2000
11

Created by Working Partners Ltd, London, W6 0QT

The moral right of the author has been asserted

Set in 14/22 Palatino

Made and printed in England by Clays Ltd, St Ives plc

British Library Cataloguing in Publication Data
A CIP catalogue record for this book is available from the British Library

ISBN 0–141–30801–X

Contents

Candelight
Rescue

Chapter One

'Sheltie! It's the Christmas holidays at last!' called Emma.

She opened the paddock gate at the bottom of the garden and rushed over to her little Shetland pony.

Sheltie was busy scratching himself on the hedge at the other side of the paddock. But as soon as he heard Emma's call, he turned his head and trotted over to meet her with a whinny of excitement.

'School finished early today,'
explained Emma, flinging her arms
round Sheltie's neck and giving him a
big hug. 'And now I've got two whole
weeks to spend with you.'

Sheltie pushed his soft muzzle into the
pocket of Emma's coat. She knew what
he was looking for. He was hoping that

there might be a treat inside for him.
Peppermints were his favourite.

'Sorry, Sheltie, no peppermints,' said
Emma, laughing. 'But I've got a carrot
for you!'

Emma searched in her bag for the
carrot treat and brought out a bundle of
bright cards instead. 'Look, Sheltie,' she
said, waving them at him. 'I've got lots
of Christmas cards from my friends.'

The little pony clearly didn't think
cards were as interesting as carrots. He
snorted and nudged at Emma's
schoolbag impatiently.

'Ah! Here's your carrot,' said Emma,
pulling it out from the bottom corner of
her bag and feeding it to the little pony.
'I'll get changed out of my school things
now and then we can ride up the lane to

celebrate the start of the Christmas holidays.'

She ran back across the paddock and into the cottage, bringing a blast of freezing air with her.

'Hello, Emma,' said Mum, smiling. There was a delicious smell of baking in the warm kitchen. 'Have a mince pie – but be careful. They're still hot.'

'Yum!' said Emma. She gave her little brother Joshua a hug and crammed a mince pie into her mouth.

'Ouch! They really *are* hot!' she cried, flapping her hands in front of her mouth. Then Emma ran upstairs to get changed. She pulled on her trousers and a bright yellow jumper and was ready in no time at all.

'I can guess where you're going,' said Mum as Emma bounced back into the kitchen.

Emma grinned, and grabbed her warm jacket and riding hat.

'It will be getting dark soon,' warned Mum, 'so don't go far.'

'I won't,' promised Emma. 'Just to the end of the lane and back.'

This time Sheltie was waiting eagerly at the paddock gate. Emma tacked him up in record time, chatting to him as she worked.

'Mum thinks it might snow, Sheltie. Wouldn't that be great?'

Sheltie snorted loudly as Emma made sure that his girth strap was tight. He seemed to like the frosty weather too. Once Emma had finished tightening the strap he pranced happily on all four legs. But as soon as Emma was up in the saddle, he calmed down and walked steadily along the lane.

As Emma and Sheltie reached Mr Crock's cottage the door opened and two faces appeared.

'What did I tell you? It's Emma and her Shetland pony,' said Mr Crock.

A little girl with brown curly hair and bright blue eyes peeped out from behind him.

'Hello, Mr Crock,' shouted Emma. 'Happy Christmas! Have you got visitors?'

'This is my granddaughter, Rosie,' said the old man. He lifted up the little girl, who looked a bit older than Emma's brother, Joshua. 'We heard you trotting

down the lane. Rosie, come and meet
Emma and Sheltie.'

Sheltie pushed his velvety muzzle
towards Rosie. He whickered softly.

'Careful, Sheltie,' warned Emma.
'Don't frighten Rosie.'

But Sheltie was always gentle. Rosie gave a cry of delight and patted Sheltie's mane. 'He's lovely!' she said.

'Rosie's staying here for Christmas,' said Mr Crock. 'Her dad has gone to America for an important conference. But he's promised to be back for Christmas day, hasn't he, Rosie?'

Rosie smiled and nodded, but Emma saw that her eyes were sad. She was obviously missing her dad. Sheltie nosed at her hair, and suddenly Rosie laughed again. 'That tickles!' she said.

Mr Crock shivered. 'It's going to freeze tonight,' he said to Emma. 'It'll snow in the next day or two, I reckon. I'd better take Rosie inside.'

Emma looked at the little girl's sad face and suddenly had an idea. 'Would you like to come to my house tomorrow, Rosie?' she asked. 'You can ride Sheltie, if you like.'

Rosie's eyes lit up. 'Can I?' she said. 'Oh, Grandad, can I?'

'Yes, of course. I know you won't come to any harm with Sheltie – he'll look after you,' said Mr Crock. 'Thank you, Emma. We'll see you tomorrow then.'

By ten o'clock the next morning Emma had already fed and groomed Sheltie. She decided to take him out for a short ride before Rosie arrived so that he wouldn't be too frisky for her. Sheltie and Emma enjoyed the ride so much that Emma didn't notice the time. As they trotted back towards the cottage she saw two pairs of boots on the doorstep. Mr Crock and Rosie must be there already. Emma dismounted and led Sheltie to the back door.

'Shall we give them a surprise?' Emma whispered to her pony.

She tiptoed to the door and Sheltie trod carefully too, though it was difficult for him to be quiet with his metal shoes. But just as Emma flung open the door, Sheltie decided to give everyone a surprise of his own.

He pushed past Emma, his hoofs clattering on the tiled floor, and made straight for the plate of mince pies on the table.

'Oh no!' cried Mum, and whipped the plate out of Sheltie's reach just in time.

'Sheltie!' shouted Emma. 'Get your

nose out of there!' She caught hold of his
bridle and tried to pull him back
outside.

'Mind your toes, Rosie,' said Mr
Crock, grinning.

Rosie giggled. Emma could see that
the little girl thought this was fun. But
she had to show Sheltie that he mustn't
behave badly. She tugged the little pony

back outside and tethered him loosely to the paddock fence. Then she raced back into the cottage.

'Do you still want to ride on such a naughty pony?' Mr Crock asked Rosie, with a twinkle in his eye.

'Oh, yes!' breathed Rosie, her eyes shining.

'He won't be naughty with Rosie, I promise,' said Emma. 'I'm sorry – I was going to creep up on you and give you a surprise, but Sheltie thought of a better one!'

'He must have smelled the mince pies,' said Mum, smiling. 'Now let's see if Joshua's hat will fit you, Rosie.'

Joshua's riding hat fitted the little girl perfectly. She went outside and pulled on her boots.

Mr Crock lifted Rosie on to Sheltie,
and Emma walked the little pony slowly
round the paddock. At first Mr Crock
held on to Rosie, but soon she was able
to sit on the saddle all by herself. Her
eyes shone with pleasure.

'Good boy, Sheltie,' praised Emma.
Sheltie turned his head towards

Emma. His warm brown eyes seemed to be saying, 'But I'm always good!'

When Emma had said goodbye to Rosie and Mr Crock she untacked Sheltie and went back inside. Mum had another visitor! It was Mrs Price, the headmaster's wife.

'We're collecting some food and decorations for the old people of Little Applewood,' Mrs Price was explaining. 'Some of them haven't got much money, and they're finding the winter very hard.'

'I've made an extra Christmas pudding,' said Mum. 'And I can do another batch of mince pies. But how are we going to deliver the gifts without people thinking we're giving out charity? Some of the old folk would hate to think we thought they couldn't cope.'

Emma thought hard. There must be
some way they could make it fun. Then
she remembered how, last Christmas,
she and her friends had paraded
through the village singing carols.

'Why don't we have a candlelit procession?' she suggested. 'I'm sure Sally and my other friends from school would love to be in it. Then we could take everyone a present – just a bag of sweets for people who don't really need anything and proper food for the people who do.'

Mrs Price looked relieved. 'What a wonderful idea, Emma!'

Chapter Two

'How are we going to carry all of this?' asked Sally. 'There are only going to be about twenty of us!' She held up a huge basketful of carrots and onions with both hands.

Emma looked at her best friend in dismay. 'You're right. And the little children will be able to carry even less. Just look at all those potatoes!'

The village hall was full of goodies.

There were mince pies, Christmas puddings and fresh vegetables and fruit. There was holly, and mistletoe, and paper decorations too.

Lots of Emma's school friends had agreed to take part in the procession. It was planned for the next evening and they were all busy packing baskets full of gifts in the village hall. But now they were faced with an even bigger problem.

'We've got to carry our lanterns as well,' pointed out Dylan.

'So that leaves just one hand to carry a basket,' said Robert.

Alice, Josie and Tracy tested how heavy the baskets were and shook their heads. *They* could just manage to carry them, but their little brothers and sisters would never be able to.

'We'll have to keep coming back for more, I suppose,' sighed Mrs Price. 'Perhaps we should forget about the lanterns.'

Emma was disappointed. The whole point of a candlelit procession was to have candles. And if they had to keep coming back to the village hall, it wouldn't be much of a procession either.

'There must be a way,' said Emma to Sally.

Emma racked her brains all evening before she went to bed. When she woke up the next morning her head was still buzzing with the problem.

I'll give Sheltie a ride, Emma said to herself. Perhaps that will help me think.

While Emma put on Sheltie's tack she

told him all about the problem. When he was ready, Emma led him through the paddock gate and past the garage door.

Suddenly, Sheltie stopped. He tossed his mane and blew a loud raspberry.

He stamped his feet and pushed his head against the garage doors. They made a loud clanking noise. Emma tugged at the pony's reins and tried to pull him away, but Sheltie simply tugged back and pawed at the doors with his hoofs.

'Don't do that, Sheltie!' said Emma. 'Mum and Dad will be cross if you scrape all the paint off. What's the matter?'

Emma pulled open the door and poked her nose inside. Sheltie poked his nose inside too and whinnied loudly. There stood Sheltie's little fish cart.

'Of course!' she said. 'We can carry the baskets around in your cart! Brilliant! Is that what you were trying to tell me, boy?'

Sheltie blew hard down his nose and Emma gave him a hug. 'You're such a clever pony, aren't you?'

Once Sheltie was out of the garage, Emma shut the doors again, tethered her pony to the fence, and ran inside to tell Mum.

'It's certainly big enough to take all the fruit and vegetables and puddings round the village,' said Mum.

'And everybody will have their hands free to carry their lanterns,' said Emma. 'The candlelit procession will happen after all!'

'That cart will need a good scrub though,' said Mum. 'Perhaps Rosie would like to help. She needs cheering up because she's missing her dad.'

Emma took Sheltie for a short ride and called in for Rosie on her way back home.

Rosie wanted Sheltie to help wash the cart too, so the three of them crowded into the garage. Emma fetched a big pail of soapy water and two sponges – one for her and one for Rosie.

Sheltie watched the two girls curiously.

He bent his head to investigate.

'Don't drink that, Sheltie!' cried Emma.

But before she could move the pail away from him, the Shetland pony blew into the water. Lots of little bubbles frothed up and clung to his mane and ears.

Rosie giggled. 'He looks funny! He's like Father Christmas, with a big white beard!' Sheltie sneezed, and bubbles floated all over the garage. Rosie laughed again, and by the time Mr Crock came to pick her up she was quite cheerful. The fish cart looked as good as new, and Emma and Rosie had even decorated it with some trailing ivy

As Emma was saying goodbye to Rosie she had another idea. 'Why don't you come with us, Rosie?'

Rosie shook her head and looked at the floor.

'There will be a lot of strange people,' explained Mr Crock. 'She gets a bit shy.'

Emma thought hard, then said, 'Will you come if you can ride Sheltie in the procession?'

Rosie's eyes sparkled. She beamed and said, 'Ride Sheltie? Oh, yes, *please!*'

Chapter Three

When everybody met at the village hall that evening it was just beginning to get dark.

Emma and her friends were putting the finishing touches to the baskets. Josie, Tracy and Alice put on their thick winter gloves and tied prickly holly to the sides. Mrs Price helped Rosie tie a ribbon on top. As soon as each basket was ready, Emma and Sally placed it in the decorated cart.

Suddenly there was a shriek from Rosie. 'Sheltie! Sheltie!'

Emma spun round.

The little pony was trotting through the hall towards them. Somehow he had managed to pull his tether rope loose from the ring outside the hall and push his way inside. Sheltie had been good all day, but Emma knew how much he hated to be left outside when there were exciting things happening. Before Emma could stop him, he had helped himself to a large carrot.

'Oh, Sheltie, how did you get free?' cried Emma. She and Sally quickly led him away from the lovely vegetables and took him back outside.

Dylan and Robert laughed so much

that they nearly fell into the cart full of
baskets. Mrs Price was cross with them.

'If you can't do anything sensible, you
two, go outside and make sure that
Sheltie doesn't sneak back in,' she said.

At last everything was ready and
Sheltie was allowed to take his position
in-between the shafts of the laden cart.

He skittered a bit on the polished floor of the hall and gave a loud, wet blow right down Rosie's neck. The little girl giggled. 'That was *yucky*, Sheltie!'

'Make sure you behave once we're out on the street,' warned Emma in her sternest voice.

Sheltie looked at her innocently through his long forelock, as if to say, 'Don't I always behave?'

By now it was really dark, but the members of the procession had their twinkling lanterns to guide them through the village. Mrs Price led the way. Rosie sat proudly on Sheltie's back, with Emma and Sally walking on each side of the little pony. Mum followed at the back of the procession to make sure that everyone was safe.

Mrs Price and Mum knew Little Applewood very well. Whenever they reached a house where an old person lived, Emma would bring Sheltie to a halt. Then she and her friends would deliver a basket of goodies.

It was easy to give out the little packets of sweets too. Nearly all of the villagers came out of their homes to watch the procession anyway, so Robert and Dylan just handed them each a packet.

'Are you having a lovely holiday with your grandad, Rosie?' asked Mrs Marsh as the procession stopped at her house.

'Yes, but my daddy will be here for Christmas too,' said Rosie bravely.

'I know, love,' said Mrs Marsh, peering eagerly into her gift basket.

Suddenly, Rosie cried out in alarm. Emma saw what her cheeky pony was up to. Sheltie was trying to turn his plump little body in the shafts. He had pushed his shaggy head round as far as it would go, and was trying to reach an apple from one of the baskets in the cart.

'Don't worry, Sheltie, I've saved you an apple for later!' said Emma kindly as she pulled at his reins.

Sally grinned across at her and Emma couldn't help giggling. Sheltie was so naughty, but so funny at the same time. She tried to look stern. 'Now then, boy, you must behave.' She clicked her tongue, and they all moved off to the next group of houses.

Everyone cheered as they watched the procession go by with its gleaming lanterns. The villagers were all thrilled with their gifts.

Finally they came to the last house in the village. This was set apart from most of the other houses. It looked very dark and lonely.

'All the lights are off,' said Emma with a frown. 'Do you think Mr Bates has gone away for Christmas?'

'Let's knock,' said Dylan. He and

Robert raced ahead and hammered at
the door.

'No answer,' they called as they came
back. 'Perhaps he's asleep.'

'Let's just go and make sure,' said
Mum. 'It won't do any harm.'

'Walk on, Sheltie,' said Emma. 'This is
the last house.'

Sheltie blew a snort and turned his
big shaggy head towards the nearly
empty cart. His eyes twinkled brightly
in the candlelight. The little pony
tossed back his hairy head so that his
bridle jingled, and gave a very loud
whinny.

'If Mr Bates was asleep he won't be
now,' said Emma, giggling as she lifted
the last basket down from the cart.

Sheltie pulled up right beside the high

windows of the cottage. Rosie peeped in from Sheltie's back.

'Oh, I can see a light!' shouted Rosie. 'It's flickering – he's got a candle like ours.'

'A candle?' said Mum quickly. 'Can you move Sheltie out of the way a

moment please, Emma, and I'll have a look.'

She stood on tiptoe and peered through the window and gasped. 'You're right, Rosie. There is just a candle,' she said. 'Poor Mr Bates is sitting wrapped in blankets. He looks very cold and lonely. I wonder what's the matter.'

Chapter Four

'Mr Bates! Mr Bates!' called Emma and
Sally together. Everyone joined in and
Sheltie added to the noise with his
loudest whinny! Rosie banged on the
window from Sheltie's back.

'Hush!' said Mrs Price. 'We won't be
able to hear him.' She pressed her ear to
the door.

Then they all heard his voice. 'I can't
open the door,' he said weakly. 'I'm too

cold to move and that'll let all the cold air in!'

'Oh dear!' said Emma anxiously. 'What can we do to help?'

'I'll see if I can get PC Green on my mobile phone,' said Mum. 'We must get in somehow.'

'Don't stand still, you lot,' called Mrs Price. 'It's too cold. Have a race to the field gate and back.'

'Me too!' said Rosie.

Mum lifted Rosie down and they all stuck their lanterns into Mr Bates' tidy front garden.

'One, two, three, GO!' shouted Mrs Price.

Everyone raced off except Emma, who stayed to look after Sheltie and the cart. Mum switched on her phone and began to tap in the policeman's number.

'Where are you going now, Sheltie?' asked Emma as her pony disappeared around the side of the cottage. She quickly followed him.

Now that he wasn't responsible for Rosie, Sheltie seemed to be very interested in the cottage. He knocked his little fish cart into the stone wall as he nudged against a small window on the side wall. An icy wind whipped round the corner and banged the window in its frame.

'The latch must be broken!' said Emma. 'No wonder poor Mr Bates is so cold. It must be really draughty in there.'

Sheltie snorted into Emma's neck and pushed her gently towards the wall. One of the cart wheels banged against the cottage again.

'Be careful, Sheltie!' cried Emma. 'We don't want to break your cart.'

But the Shetland pony wouldn't stop nudging at Emma. Finally he lifted his shaggy head as if to point to the window and blew a loud raspberry.

'Wait a minute ...' said Emma slowly. 'I think I could fit through that window. I wonder what's on the other side. Stand still, boy, while I get up and look.'

She hauled herself up on to Sheltie's back, and the little pony stood as steady as a rock beneath her. Emma pushed at the window, and it opened a little way. There was just enough space for her to wriggle through.

Mum had finished her call to PC

Green and came to see what Emma was
trying to do. 'Emma, be careful!' she
said. 'You mustn't try climbing through
there!'

'It's all right, Mum,' said Emma.
'There's a sofa right underneath. I'll be
quite safe.' Then she called through the
window to Mr Bates. 'I'm going to come
in and help you, Mr Bates! Don't be
frightened.'

Sheltie stood very still while Emma
grabbed hold of the window frame and
squeezed herself
through head first.

Then she carefully wriggled down towards the comfy sofa.

'Easy-peasy!' she said, and with a final wriggle she tumbled in a heap on to the sofa cushions. Sheltie gave a high, excited whinny from outside.

'It's all right, Mr Bates,' said Emma, rushing over to where he was sitting wrapped in blankets.

Mr Bates managed a smile. 'I've run out of money for the electricity meter,' he mumbled. 'I've run out of wood too – and it's so cold, I just couldn't bear to go outside to get some more. I didn't want to let you in either, because of the cold air. I – I thought I'd never get warm again if I did that.'

'We've come to help,' said Emma. 'We've got a special Christmas food

basket for you, and we can bring in
some logs for your fire. I won't open the
door very far,' promised Emma, 'but I'm
going to let Mum in.'

She unbolted the front door and Mum
squeezed through, trying not to let in
too much cold air.

Emma quickly explained to Mum why there were no lights or heating, and Mum put some coins in the meter. Suddenly the lights came on, and there was a cheer from outside. All the other children had come back from their run and were waiting in the front garden.

'Why haven't you phoned your daughter, Mr Bates?' asked Mum. 'She lives near by, doesn't she? I'm sure she'd have come and helped.'

'She's got the flu, and the children are poorly too,' said Mr Bates stubbornly. 'I don't want to be a nuisance.'

'She won't think you're a nuisance,' said Mum. 'Nobody should be on their own at this time of year. Let me ring her, and you can have a chat. But first I'm going to phone PC Green and tell him you're all right.'

Emma opened the door a little way, and everyone crowded in. Mrs Price brought in the last few baskets of goodies. It was such a squash inside Mr Bates' cottage that it began to feel warm immediately. Emma nipped back outside to tether Sheltie to a tree. Tracy and Sally brought in armfuls of logs and Mum soon coaxed the fire to burn brightly.

Then Mum talked to Mr Bates' daughter on the phone. She was horrified that her father had said nothing about his problems. She said she would come over straight away and take Mr Bates home for Christmas.

'Your grandchildren are feeling better

now,' Mum explained to Mr Bates with a smile. 'Your daughter will be here in an hour.'

Mr Bates grinned with relief.

'An hour? Great!' shouted Robert. 'We can have a party here while we're waiting!'

The fire was roaring up the chimney now, and there were mince pies, Christmas cake and oranges to eat. Sally and Tracy hung paper decorations over the walls, while Dylan and Robert tried to tuck holly behind the pictures without pricking themselves. Mum phoned everyone's parents on her mobile to explain why they were going to be a bit late home.

'I didn't expect a party,' laughed Mr Bates, his mouth full of mince pie.

'It's all thanks to Sheltie,' said Emma.
'He found the open window.'

'I wish there was room for him in
here,' said Rosie sadly.

Sheltie obviously agreed. He had
managed to pull his tether rope free and
was kicking rather loudly at the front
door! Emma opened it just a little way.

Everybody burst out laughing when

Sheltie's furry head peered into the room. His eyes twinkled with fun as he looked round at all his friends. Then he blew a very loud raspberry.

'Well, this *is* a different Christmas!' said Mr Bates, laughing. 'I've never had a Shetland pony stopping up the draughts before!'

A Christmas Star

Chapter One

'Look at Sheltie!' said Rosie, laughing.
'He's so funny!'

'Oh no!' cried Emma. She rushed over
to the other side of the village hall just
before Sheltie knocked some scenery
over. 'Sheltie, you're messing everything
up!' she said.

After all the excitement of the
candlelit procession, the younger
children of Little Applewood had to

carry on rehearsing for the nativity play. This was going to be held in the village hall on Christmas Eve. Mrs Price, who was organizing the play, had asked some of the older children to help with the costumes and scenery, and Sally and Emma had brought Rosie along with them. The little girl had insisted that Sheltie come inside too.

'Stay here, Sheltie, where I can keep an eye on you,' said Emma. She led the pony closer to where she and Sally were working on some paper crowns for the Three Kings.

Sheltie seemed very interested in the gold and silver paper lying on the floor. He grabbed at a length with his strong teeth and flicked it over his shaggy head. He pulled at another length and

managed to wind it round his thick
neck. Then he pawed at a heap of stripy
clothes and soon his legs were all
tangled up in them! Sheltie looked
rather funny with paper draped over
him and his legs tangled up in a
shepherd costume!

'Sorry, Rosie. We'll have to take him

outside,' said Emma. 'He's just too naughty to be in here.' She could see that Rosie was upset. When Sheltie was around the little girl seemed to forget about her dad not being there.

Emma took Sheltie outside and tethered him to the railings by the door. It was then that she had an idea.

'Perhaps Rosie could be in the play,' she suggested to Sally. 'Mrs Price,' she called, 'can Rosie be a shepherd?'

'What a good idea,' said Mrs Price. 'I've got an extra costume.'

But Rosie didn't seem sure about being a shepherd, even when Emma said that her little brother, Joshua, was going to be a shepherd too.

'Mudlark!' said Joshua, making a funny *hee haw* noise.

'Oh yes! Joshua has just reminded me,' said Emma. 'Marjorie Wallace, Mudlark's owner, said we could borrow him because we need a donkey in the play. In fact, Mudlark will be coming to the dress rehearsal tomorrow,' Emma went on. 'So, Rosie, would you like to be a shepherd now?'

Rosie looked very excited. She loved animals. 'Yes, please!' she said.

It was Christmas Eve. Emma and Sheltie called for Rosie on their way to the morning dress rehearsal.

But Rosie had changed her mind about being a shepherd. 'I want to stay at home in case Daddy comes,' she said.

'Her dad's been delayed because of the bad weather,' explained Mr Crock.

Then he turned to Rosie. 'You don't want to miss being in the play,' he said to the little girl. 'Everyone's coming to watch you tonight.'

Sheltie threw back his shaggy head and blew a loud raspberry. Rosie giggled.

'Sheltie wants you to come,' said

Emma. 'And remember, Mudlark will be there too.'

Rosie's eyes gleamed as she remembered Mudlark. 'OK, I'll come,' she said. 'But can I give Sheltie a carrot first?'

Mr Crock's eyes twinkled. 'Keep him away from my vegetables,' he said gruffly to Emma as he went inside to fetch a carrot for the pony. Mr Crock was very proud of his garden. Even in the freezing cold there were Brussels sprouts growing in his neat vegetable beds.

Sheltie took the carrot gently between his lips and blew softly into Rosie's outstretched palm. His dark eyes twinkled through the mass of hair over his face.

Emma helped Rosie to put on Joshua's riding hat, then Mr Crock lifted the little girl on to Sheltie's back and they were off.

'Walk on gently, Sheltie,' said Emma.

Sheltie stepped out proudly as if Rosie were a little princess on his back. He didn't seem to need Emma to tell him what to do!

'Can Sheltie come in?' asked Rosie when they reached the hall. She slid off his back by herself, with Emma watching to make sure she didn't stumble when she reached the ground. Sheltie turned to Emma and looked at her with his big brown eyes.

'No, Sheltie, there are too many things to knock over inside,' said Emma firmly. 'Would you like to help me take his saddle off and tether him to the railings, Rosie?' She showed Rosie the special knot that she used to loosely tether the pony.

Once they were back inside Rosie soon forgot about Sheltie. There was so much to do.

Emma and Sally had to make sure that all the actors were wearing the right costumes and standing in the right place. Then they took their places on either side of the stage. It was their job to draw the curtains at the beginning and end of each scene. They were only missing one actor now ... Mudlark.

'Marjorie promised she'd be here in time,' said Mrs Price. 'We're half an hour late already. I suppose we'll just have to start without the donkey.'

Emma was worried. It wasn't like
Marjorie to be late. Emma hoped that
there was nothing wrong.

Suddenly, the doors of the hall burst
open. It was Marjorie at last. But where
was Mudlark? There hadn't even been a

whinny from outside. Surely Sheltie
would have greeted his old friend?

Mrs Price stopped the rehearsal and
hurried over.

'I'm so sorry, everyone,' gasped
Marjorie. She was panting as if she had
been running. 'Mudlark's gone lame. I
only found out this morning, so it was
too late to phone you, Mrs Price. It's not
serious, but I'm afraid you won't have a
donkey for Mary to ride in the play!'

Chapter Two

Everyone crowded round as Marjorie
explained about Mudlark.

'He was fine yesterday,' she said. 'But
some time early this morning he must
have slipped on an icy patch outside his
shed and twisted his foreleg.'

Poor Mudlark! thought Emma.

Marjorie told them that the donkey's
knee was badly swollen, and the vet had
said Mudlark would be out of action for

the next few days. They couldn't borrow Sophie, Marjorie's other donkey, either. Her brother Todd had taken Sophie to visit friends for the day, and wouldn't be back until late.

'Never mind,' said Mrs Price briskly to the children. 'Mudlark's going to be all right, that's the main thing. And we don't really need a donkey. Mary will just have to walk.'

'It won't be the same, Mrs Price!' said Wayne, who was playing Joseph. They had all been looking forward to having a donkey in their play.

After Emma had said goodbye to Marjorie, she turned to find Rosie by her side.

'Go on, Rosie,' she said gently. 'You've got to go and be a shepherd now.'

'I wish Mudlark was here,' Rosie
sighed, and walked slowly back to join
the rest of the shepherds. Just then there
was a loud whinny from outside.

'Sheltie!' exclaimed Emma, and
rushed outside.

Sheltie was shaking his head backwards and forwards and yanking at his tether rope. When he saw Emma, he gave another great whinny.

'Sheltie, what's the matter? Has someone been teasing you?' cried Emma. She looked up and down the village street, but there was no one to be seen.

Sheltie neighed and tossed his shaggy mane so that it flew round his head like a great dandelion clock. Then he pawed at the ground and pulled hard on his tether rope again.

'Are you just making a fuss because you can't come inside?' said Emma. She put her arms round his neck and hugged him. 'Calm down, boy. The rehearsal won't take long now.'

But Sheltie didn't seem to want to calm down. He kept on shaking his head and pulling at his tether rope as if he was trying to get in through the doors of the hall.

'You know you can't go in there,' said Emma firmly. 'You'll distract Mudlark from his job …'

And then she suddenly remembered. Of course! Mudlark wasn't in the hall, and there was no donkey for the Christmas play. Perhaps Sheltie could take Mudlark's place … After all, he had drawn Cinderella's coach in their school pantomime last year. He was a good actor, but would he behave himself? It was worth a try.

'Come on then, boy,' she whispered. 'Let's go and tell everyone that Mary can ride to the stable on a Shetland pony instead of on a donkey!'

Emma led the little pony into the hall. All the actors clapped their hands and cheered when Emma suggested that Sheltie could take Mudlark's place. But Mrs Price wasn't so sure.

'I seem to remember that Sheltie doesn't always behave himself,' she said uncertainly. 'We don't want him eating the scenery.'

But everyone else protested.

'He'll be a brilliant donkey, Mrs Price,' said Wayne.

'I'm sure he'll be good,' said Rosie anxiously. She really wanted Sheltie to be on stage with her.

'All right then,' said Mrs Price at last. 'But you must look after him, Emma.

Put his saddle back on and make sure he behaves. The first time he nibbles a costume he's out!'

Sheltie looked at Mrs Price and slowly blinked his dark, twinkly eyes. He walked up to the stage, as good as gold, and climbed on to the low platform. Then he turned round and shook his mane gently as if to say, 'There! Didn't I do that well?'

Mrs Price lifted the little girl playing Mary on to Sheltie's back. The pony stood still as a rock for her.

Rosie tugged at Emma's hand. 'Can I lead him?' she whispered.

'I don't think a shepherd would lead a donkey,' said Emma, worried.

But Mrs Price had heard Rosie too. 'As you've been learning how to look after

Sheltie, Rosie,' she said, 'how would you like to be the innkeeper's daughter, instead of a shepherd? Then you can show Mary's donkey where the stable is.'

Rosie went pink and nodded her head. Sheltie blew gently down his nose and nodded his shaggy head too.

Emma showed Rosie how to hold on to Sheltie's reins and lead him. The Shetland pony behaved perfectly. He walked slowly across the stage with Mary on his back and stopped right by the manger. Sheltie waited until Emma and Sally drew the curtains across to end the scene, then stretched out his neck towards the sweet hay.

'No, Sheltie,' said Rosie in a stern voice. She sounded just like Emma when

she was trying to be strict with Sheltie.
This made Emma giggle. Rosie was
doing a very good job with the little
pony.

The next scene was set after the baby

was born. Once the children had sung a carol, Mary was supposed to put the baby down into the manger. But Mary couldn't quite reach the manger from her chair. Mrs Price rushed up on to the stage to push the manger forward.

As the teacher was bending over the crib, Sheltie turned his head and gave her bottom a sly nudge. The children couldn't help laughing.

'Sheltie! You naughty pony!' said Mrs Price crossly.

Emma gave Sheltie a scolding.

'If you don't behave I'll have to take you home,' she told him severely.

The Shetland pony hung his head as if he was sorry. Then he lifted it up and blew a long, loud raspberry that made everyone laugh again.

When Emma saw the mischievous glint in his eye she knew there could be more trouble to come!

Chapter Three

'There'll never be time to do everything!'
cried Emma once she was back at the
cottage that afternoon. 'I want to take
Sheltie for a ride, even if it's a short
one. If he doesn't have some exercise
he'll run around and do something
naughty during the play. Then I've got
to have my tea, then clean Sheltie's
hoofs –'

'And after all that you've got to hang

up your stocking!' interrupted Dad with a smile.

'Oh, yes!' said Emma, clapping her hand to her head. 'There's so much to do I'd forgotten it was Christmas day tomorrow!'

'Calm down, Emma,' said Mum. 'You can have a quick sandwich now. The play won't go on very late so we can eat properly when we come back. And I'm afraid you really can't go for a ride. The weather forecast says that heavy snow is coming. It's already started – look.'

Emma looked out of the cottage window. Flakes of snow were swirling round over Sheltie's paddock. 'Wow! We're going to have a white Christmas after all!' she said happily.

She did have time to give her little

pony a brush down. He still had bits of
gold and silver paper stuck in his mane
from the dress rehearsal. Emma brushed
hard, but there was no way Sheltie could
ever look really tidy.

'It's a good job you're supposed to be
a donkey and not a show pony, Sheltie,'
she told him. She leant against his fat

little tummy so that she could lift his leg and work at the feathery tufts above one of his hoofs.

Sheltie stamped his hoof against the ground when she let it down. Then he lifted the next leg for her to brush with no trouble at all.

'Good boy, Sheltie. I hope you behave as well as this in the play,' said Emma.

Sheltie looked at her with his melting brown eyes. Emma flung her arms round his neck, burying her face in his shaggy mane. 'I'm sorry, Sheltie. I know you're going to be the best actor in the play tonight!'

The village hall was packed. Everybody in Little Applewood had come to see the Christmas play. Emma saw lots of

her friends. There was Mrs Pinkerton
from the corner shop, Charlie from the
garage and Mr Samson from the sweet
shop. Mr Crock sat in the front row
with Emma's mum and dad and Sally's
parents. When Rosie led Sheltie on to
the stage with Mary on his back Mr
Crock clapped very loudly. But Rosie
didn't look at him once. She kept
looking straight ahead of her, just like
Emma had told her.

'Whoa, Sheltie,' she said, and Sheltie
stopped straight away. After Mrs Price
had lifted Mary down from the little
pony, Rosie led Sheltie to stand behind
the manger.

Emma kept an eye on Sheltie from
where she was standing by the curtain –
just in case. Sheltie looked back at her

with a twinkle in his eye. He stood as
still as a statue.

At the end of the performance, all the
actors bowed, and everybody clapped
and cheered. Sheltie stood patiently
behind the actors, waiting for everybody
to finish bowing.

It was a long time for a little pony to
stand still. And nobody had asked
Sheltie to come forward to take a bow.
Emma was just wondering whether she
ought to go and bring him forward
when suddenly the Shetland pony
pushed his way gently through the
children. He stopped just behind the
manger.

'Isn't he clever!' cried someone in the
audience as Sheltie bent his head in a
bow.

But Emma could see what Sheltie was really trying to do. She hissed to Sally, 'Close the curtains! Quick!'

Sally looked at Sheltie and quickly drew her curtain. But she couldn't help laughing. The pony wasn't bowing at all. His head was bent into the manger, and he was stealing a mouthful of hay from underneath the doll baby!

While all the children and the audience ate their feast of mince pies and Christmas cake, Emma took off Sheltie's saddle and gave Rosie a peppermint to palm to him as a special reward.

'He was very good *nearly* all the time,' said Emma. She gave the little pony a big hug.

Sheltie nuzzled Rosie as if to say that they were a great team.

Gradually the villagers began to put on their coats and scarves and hats. Mrs Price, Emma and Sally packed the costumes in a big box to take back to school after Christmas. It was time for everyone to go home and hang up their stockings.

Emma's dad went to open the hall doors. But when he tried to push them open, they wouldn't budge!

'Has somebody locked the door?' he asked.

He pushed again and the doors opened just a little way. A huge blast of icy wind came into the hall. Through the crack, Emma and Dad could see a great white wall of snow!

Chapter Four

'Wow!' gasped Emma. The wall of snow was almost as high as Sheltie.

'What are we going to do?' said Dad anxiously. 'It looks as though the wind's blown all the snow against the hall doors.'

'A snowdrift!' said Mr Crock, peering over Dad's shoulder.

'We'll soon shove our way out,' said Charlie from the garage confidently. 'We just need a few strong people.'

Sally's dad came forward, and so did several other people.

'Push, everyone,' ordered Charlie. 'All together now – one, two, *three!*'

Mr Samson, Charlie, Mr Jones, Dad and the others all shoved hard. But outside the doors the snow had piled up

so thickly that pushing just seemed to pack it tighter.

'How are we all going to get home?' cried Mrs Pinkerton.

Everybody crowded round the doors and tried to help push. But the doors still only opened a little way and there wasn't room for even the smallest person to squeeze through.

Some of the younger children began to cry. Emma knew that they must be wondering how they would get home to hang up their stockings for Santa.

'Sssh!' said Mrs Jones, trying to comfort them. 'They'll dig us out soon, you'll see.'

Suddenly, Sheltie charged towards the crowd of people.

'Sheltie, come back!' cried Emma in

alarm. She raced to grab hold of his
bridle, but Sheltie was already in the
middle of the crowd.

'Hey, stop that!' shouted Mr Crock.
'You nearly trod on my toes!'

Lots of other people shouted too, but
Sheltie didn't stop. He kept on barging
his way through the crowd until he had
reached Dad and Emma. And he didn't
even stop there. He went on, right to the
hall doors.

Emma realized what Sheltie was
doing and grinned.

'Don't worry,' she said to the villagers.
'Sheltie's going to push his way out!'

'Don't be silly!' said Mrs Pinkerton.
'He's only a tiny pony. He can't possibly
do anything.'

'He may be little, but he's very

strong,' said Emma. 'If anyone can do it,
he will.' Don't let me down now, boy!
she thought, willing Sheltie to push
open the hall doors.

Sheltie stopped in front of the doors as
if considering what to do next. The fierce
wind whistled in and blew the pony's

shaggy hair right over his ears. Icy snow sprayed in too. Dad jumped back so that he didn't get covered in it.

The little pony pawed at the doors, his hoofs slipping on the shiny paint. Then he pushed his body against the doors, but he still couldn't open them.

'There you are, I told you,' said Mrs Pinkerton.

Sheltie moved back a little bit and Charlie dodged out of the way of his back hoofs. 'Good try, boy,' he said. 'Come on, lads, let's have another go.'

But Sheltie wasn't finished yet. He moved back another step, then charged forwards with all his might.

'Go, Sheltie, go!' whispered Emma. 'You can do it, I know you can!'

The pony's powerful shoulders

pressed against the doors and forced them to open just a little bit more. There was enough room for Sheltie to push his way out now. This meant that there would also be room for people to get out of the hall ... but they wouldn't be able to go very far. There was still a great wall of snow ahead.

'Oh, clever Sheltie! I knew you could do it,' breathed Emma. 'Well done, boy!'

She waited anxiously to see what the pony would do next. All the villagers watched and waited too. Sheltie ploughed steadily through the wall of snow with his strong little legs. Emma felt so proud of him.

Very soon Sheltie had trampled down enough snow for people to escape. He

had walked right through the snowdrift
and cleared a narrow path.

'Three cheers for Sheltie!' yelled
Charlie. 'Now we can all go home and
wait for Santa!'

The villagers cheered and whistled.

'Three cheers for Sheltie! Happy Christmas, everyone!'

Once everyone had got past the drifts piled up against the village hall, the snow wasn't so bad. But all the people who had come by car had to leave their cars behind and walk home. Rosie begged to ride home on Sheltie. Emma saddled Sheltie up again and Mr Crock lifted his granddaughter on to the brave pony. Emma led the two of them back through the village with Mum, Dad and Joshua following behind.

It had stopped snowing now, but everything was white. Emma thought the houses looked just like iced cakes. Snow squeaked gently under Sheltie's hoofs, but Emma couldn't hear anyone else's footsteps at all.

As they turned into the lane Emma said, 'Look, everyone – there's a star.'

In the night sky there was a single bright star.

'Let's all make a wish,' said Mum.

The little procession stopped and everyone looked up at the magical star. Emma closed her eyes. What should she wish for? There were so many things!

New stirrup leathers for Sheltie? The old ones were getting very worn. A year's supply of pony nuts? Or to have lots more fun and adventures with Sheltie next year? It was just too difficult.

She opened her eyes and looked at Rosie on Sheltie's back. The little girl's eyes were shut tight. Emma knew exactly what she was wishing for. She wanted her dad to be home in time for Christmas.

Now Emma knew what her own wish was going to be. She shut her eyes and wished for exactly the same as Rosie.

Then Rosie opened her eyes and gave Emma a huge grin.

Somehow Emma was certain that their wish was going to come true.

Wish Come True

Chapter One

Emma woke up to brilliant sunshine.

'Oh no!' she cried. 'I must have overslept!'

And then she remembered.

It was Christmas Day! And it was so bright because of the snow, which had arrived just in time to make it a white Christmas.

Emma found a knobbly stocking at the bottom of her bed. She couldn't hear a sound from the rest of the house. Not even from Joshua's room. How could everyone still be asleep on such a special day! But she knew she could rely on someone to be awake and waiting for her, whatever the time or weather.

Emma pulled back the curtains. Sure

enough, there was Sheltie at the paddock gate, his breath puffing out in clouds in the frosty air.

The little pony was covered with snow. He looked like a snow pony. But Sheltie never felt the cold. His thick shaggy coat was made for weather like this. And after shoving his way through the snowdrift last night, it was easy for him to trample through the snow from his field shelter to the gate.

'Happy Christmas, Sheltie,' Emma called in a whisper. 'Since you're the only one up, you can have your Christmas present first!'

Emma dressed quickly in her warmest clothes, and tiptoed downstairs to the back door. Sheltie's stocking was waiting by her boots and padded jacket. It was just as knobbly as her own. Inside there was a new head collar, and a mixture of carrots, apples and peppermint treats.

'Sheltie, you're going to love your presents,' said Emma softly as she pulled on her boots. She opened the back door and stumbled through the deep snow to the paddock gate. Sheltie blew an excited whinny as soon as he saw her.

Emma climbed over the gate, brushing the snow off the top. Then she draped Sheltie's stocking carefully over the fence.

'Isn't this lovely?' she said, flinging her arms round her snowy pony's neck. 'Just wait and see what I've got for you. But first you must have some proper breakfast.'

Sheltie loved the wintry weather. He shook his mane hard so that soft lumps of snow flew into Emma's face.

'Ouch!' said Emma as the freezing stuff hit her. 'So you want a game, do you?' She bent to scoop up a ball of snow in each hand and threw them at Sheltie's broad back. Sheltie shied away, dodging the snowballs and whinnying with delight. The pony was just too quick for Emma.

'Got you!' she laughed, as one of her snowballs finally caught Sheltie on the rump.

They played for a bit longer until Emma said, 'That's four to me, and probably about a million to you. Breakfast time!'

Sheltie seemed to know what that

meant. He quickly followed the trail of
hoof prints back to his shelter. Emma
ran after him.

'There – one measure and a tiny bit for
luck,' she told Sheltie as she scooped the
pony nuts into his feeding manger.
Sheltie plunged his head down and
munched through the lot in seconds.

The water trough had a thick layer of
ice on it. Emma bashed at the ice with a

trowel so that Sheltie could get at the water.

'You'd better have a long drink now, before it ices over again,' she told him.

Emma looked back at her cottage. All the curtains were closed, except for hers. 'Everyone's still asleep, Sheltie,' she said as the little pony drank greedily from his trough. 'How can they sleep in on Christmas Day? I wonder if we're the only people in the world awake and ready to open our presents – Oh, I nearly forgot ...' Emma raced back to the gate to fetch Sheltie's stocking. The Shetland pony looked at his stocking with great interest and tried to bite it. Then he nuzzled at it. He could obviously smell the peppermints!

'Since it's Christmas you can have a

treat for breakfast,' said Emma, fishing out the mints from the top of his stocking. She took a shiny apple out of the stocking as well, and put it into her pocket to give to him later. Then she fixed on his new head collar.

'Do you think Rosie's dad arrived last night?' she asked Sheltie.

The pony blew a long, wet raspberry, and dribbled peppermint juice on to her hand.

Emma decided she and Sheltie might as well go and see if Rosie's dad was back. If he wasn't there, at least they could give Rosie her present to cheer her up.

Emma went back inside the cottage to grab Rosie's present and to check that

nobody was awake yet. Then she led
Sheltie up the lane in his new head
collar.

As they approached Mr Crock's
cottage, Emma saw smoke rising from
Mr Crock's cottage chimney. At least
someone was up.

Mr Crock opened the door to Emma and shook his head sadly.

Oh dear, thought Emma. Rosie's dad can't be back yet.

Rosie peeped out from behind her grandad and waved at Sheltie.

'Happy Christmas, Rosie,' said Emma, and handed her a brightly wrapped parcel.

Rosie loved her toy Shetland pony, and decided to call it Sheltie. She smiled bravely, but her eyes were sad.

Suddenly, Mr Crock's phone rang in the hall. Rosie rushed to stand by her grandad as he answered it.

'It's Daddy for you!' said Mr Crock, handing Rosie the phone with a grin.

Emma watched anxiously as Rosie spoke to her dad. Finally the little girl put the phone down and gave Emma a huge grin. Her dad was on his way, and should be home in time for Christmas lunch!

Chapter Two

'They're awake at last, Sheltie!' cried
Emma as she arrived home and saw that
all the curtains were open. She flung her
arms round the little pony's neck in
excitement.

Sheltie stomped in the snow and blew
down his nose. His breath puffed out
like a cloud in the frosty air.

'After we've opened our presents I'll
come out to see you again,' Emma

promised. She undid the bolt of the gate and let Sheltie back into his paddock. She quickly took off his new head collar, dashed back to the house and pulled off her snowy boots.

'Happy Christmas, everybody!' said Emma as she burst in through the back door.

Mum, Dad, Emma and Joshua opened their presents together. It was very exciting and Emma was delighted with all her new things. She played with Joshua all morning.

After eating a delicious Christmas lunch, Emma decided to go and give Sheltie another of his Christmas treats. Sheltie munched his apple happily and then pushed at the gate. He seemed keen to go for another ride.

'The snow's a bit deep. I don't think Mum and Dad will let us go out on the downs in case we fall into a snowdrift,' said Emma. 'But I don't suppose they'll mind if we go and check again to see whether Rosie's dad's arrived.'

Emma dashed back inside to tell Mum and Dad where she was going, and then tacked up Sheltie as fast as she could in the freezing cold. Her fingers were stiff so it was difficult to do up the buckles. Then she undid the bolt, opened the gate and let Sheltie through.

The little pony trotted down the lane. Emma found it a bit tricky riding him through the slippery snow.

'Whoa, Sheltie!' she gasped. 'Slow down! We're not in a race!'

But Sheltie seemed to think he was.

He didn't slow down until they reached
Mr Crock's cottage. He nosed
impatiently at the gate. Emma let the
little pony through as quickly as she
could. As she was closing the gate
behind them, Sheltie trotted up the path
and took the door knocker in his teeth.

Almost immediately, Rosie opened the
door. She was in tears. Her dad still
hadn't arrived.

She came out to stroke Sheltie. The
Shetland pony seemed to sense that she
was upset. He gave soft little whickers
and snorts, and rubbed his fuzzy nose
into Rosie's hair.

'I'm sure he'll be here very soon,' said
Emma. 'I tell you what, would you like
Sheltie to take you for a Christmas ride?
Mum and Dad won't mind if we just go

down the village street. I'll ride home
and check with them.'

Rosie grinned. It was the next best
thing to having her dad back!

Emma urged Sheltie to trot home.
Mum and Dad agreed that a little ride
on Sheltie might take Rosie's mind off
her dad.

'Poor Rosie,' said Mum. 'She must be

very disappointed. What a good thing she's fallen in love with Sheltie! Here – don't forget to take Joshua's riding hat with you.'

Emma grabbed the riding hat and ran back out to Sheltie. Together they crunched through the snow, back up the lane.

But when they arrived at the house Rosie wasn't ready to go. The little girl had had some bad news. Mr Crock told Emma what had happened.

'Rosie's dad's has just phoned us on his mobile phone,' said Mr Crock. He looked anxious. 'He got very near Little Applewood, and then his car skidded into a snowdrift. Since he was so close, he decided to abandon it and try to walk here. But everything looks so different in the snow, and now he doesn't know where he is or which way to go. He's completely lost!'

Chapter Three

'What shall we do?' gasped Emma.
'Shall I ask Dad to get the car out?'

'I don't think he'll be able to drive it
through the snow,' said Mr Crock. 'I
think we'll just have to get our boots on
and walk! I've called PC Green. He's out
on a job at the moment, but he'll come
and help as soon as he can.'

'I'll go and fetch Mum and Dad. I'm
sure they'll want to help too,' said Emma.

Sheltie neighed as she pulled him round and urged him on with her heels. But he seemed to know that Emma was in a hurry. He trotted as quickly and carefully as he could over the snowy ground.

Before Emma had gone very far she heard a car driving up the lane towards her. She brought Sheltie to a stop to let it pass.

'Oh dear, hurry up,' said Emma to herself. 'We need to move fast before Rosie's dad freezes in the snow.'

But it was Mr Brown the farmer, in his Land Rover. As soon as she saw him, Emma realized that he might be able to help. His Land Rover moved easily over the snow. It was made for difficult roads. Perhaps the farmer

could help them search for Rosie's
dad.

Emma waved frantically at Mr Brown.

The farmer stopped his Land Rover
and wound down his window. 'Is
something wrong?' he said.

Emma quickly explained about
Rosie's dad, and Mr Brown agreed to
help search for him in the Land Rover.

'You and Sheltie can trot along beside

the Land Rover and help. Sheltie can investigate the snow drifts,' he said. 'Ponies have good noses.'

'I hope Rosie's dad isn't stuck in a drift!' said Emma anxiously.

'Don't worry,' said Mr Brown. 'If he is, at least he'll be out of this cold wind!'

A few minutes later, Emma burst into the kitchen, pink cheeked and panting.

Sheltie clattered in after her, leaving snowy hoof prints on the tiles. For once, Mum and Dad didn't mind because they could see how upset Emma was.

'He's lost in the snow!' gasped Emma. 'But Mr Brown will help!'

'Just a minute, Emma,' said Mum. 'I know you're in a hurry, but sit down for a minute and tell us all about it calmly.'

Sheltie whickered quietly and pushed his nose into Emma's hair, as if he agreed with Mum.

Emma gulped and started again, explaining about Mr Crock's phone call and how she had met Mr Brown in the lane.

'So Mr Brown's going to pick up Rosie

and Mr Crock and we'll all go and look for her dad,' Emma finished in a rush. 'If that's all right,' she added.

'That seems very sensible,' said Dad. 'I've got another idea. Why don't I go to Mr Crock's house and stay by the telephone? If Rosie's dad phones again I can give him Mr Brown's mobile number. He might be able to describe something near him that one of you recognizes.'

'You mean, like the shape of a hill or a clump of trees?' asked Emma.

'Exactly!' said Dad.

Emma tried hard not to be impatient while Dad put on his thick sweater and boots. She led Sheltie outside and sat in his saddle so that they could go as soon as Dad was ready.

Mr Crock was looking even more anxious when they arrived. Emma soon found out why.

'I've just tried Rosie's dad's mobile number, but there's no reply,' he said.

'Never mind,' said Dad cheerfully. 'I'll stay by the phone and let you know in case he does try to get in touch again. I'll also be able to give Mr Brown's number to PC Green when he phones. Then he can get in touch too, and come and help you straight away.'

Rosie looked sad and frightened as Mr Brown helped her into the Land Rover.

'Cheer up,' said Mr Crock gruffly as he climbed in after her. 'We'll find him, don't worry.'

'Sheltie will find him,' promised Emma, giving Rosie a quick hug

through the open door of the Land
Rover. Then she climbed back on to
Sheltie's saddle and waited for Mr
Brown to decide which way to go.

'Right, Emma, this way first, I think,'
said Mr Brown, pointing towards the
road that led to Fox Hall Manor, where
Emma's best friend Sally lived. 'He'll

have turned off the motorway and driven towards Beacon Hill and Little Applewood, over the downs.'

Mr Crock agreed.

Sheltie seemed to take his job very seriously. As they plodded along by the side of the Land Rover he pushed his sensitive nose into every snowdrift that they passed.

'Good boy, Sheltie,' whispered Emma. 'If anyone can find him, you can.' She pulled the reins gently to show him a new snowdrift, but Sheltie had already seen it and was crossing the road to investigate. He looked so funny with his fat tummy brushing against the deep snow! Emma saw Rosie smiling inside the Land Rover, and was glad that Sheltie was keeping the little girl happy.

The Land Rover's engine sounded very noisy in the still air. The road was empty. The fields were empty. Even the woods looked as though no one had entered them for years.

Then, suddenly, when they were halfway to Barrow Hill, Emma yelled out, 'There's a car!' She could just see the back end of it sticking out into the road at the bottom of the dip.

She urged Sheltie forward. The little pony shook his mane and his bridle jingled. He snorted loudly and Emma felt the icy wind rush past her face as Sheltie lifted his hoofs high above the thick snow to trot towards the car.

The car was half buried in a snowdrift with its nose in the hedge – just as Rosie's dad had described. But Rosie's

dad had left the car to walk the rest of
the way to Little Applewood. He could
be anywhere by now!

'This is no weather to be out in,' said
Mr Brown quietly to Emma. 'I hope we
find him soon.'

'I'm sure we will,' said Emma
confidently. But she didn't feel at all
sure. She could see Rosie's face through
the Land Rover window, looking
anxious again. Emma knew that if

Rosie's dad had walked towards Little Applewood they would have passed him by now.

'He must have gone the wrong way, back towards the downs,' said Mr Crock. 'Let's move on.'

Emma clicked her tongue to tell Sheltie to move on, but the little pony shook his head sideways and tugged at his reins. They were next to an opening in the hedge. It led to a bridle path, then through to open meadows. It was one of Sheltie's favourite rides.

'No, Sheltie,' said Emma firmly. 'We've got a job to do. We need to keep together if we're going to find Rosie's dad. He wouldn't have gone that way.'

But Sheltie whinnied loudly and stomped with his hoofs so that snow

flew up into his shaggy coat. He pulled
hard at his reins, and Emma found it
difficult to hold him. She was red in the
face from trying to stop him moving
towards the bridle path when Mr Brown
put his head out of the car window.

'Are you OK?' he asked.

'Yes –' began Emma. Then she
stopped. 'Sheltie seems to want to go
this way, over the fields. Maybe he
knows something we don't,' she said
excitedly.

'Are there any footprints?' asked Mr
Brown.

But the wind had blown snow over
any footprints that might have been
there.

'It's all right,' said Emma. 'I know the
shape of the hills. I won't get lost. And

Sheltie can find his way back from anywhere!'

Mr Crock nodded from inside the car. 'Emma's sensible,' he muttered. Then said aloud, 'Go on, see what Sheltie can do.'

The Shetland pony didn't need any encouragement from Emma. He was off with a spray of snow from his hind legs.

Sheltie seemed to know exactly where he was going, so Emma let him have his head. If she hadn't been so worried she would have enjoyed the exciting gallop over the fields in the deep snow.

Emma kept looking over at the hedges, just in case Rosie's dad was sheltering there, but there was no sign of anyone moving about.

Suddenly Sheltie slowed to a stop.

'Have you found something, boy?' asked Emma quietly. She held the reins loosely in her lap, so that Sheltie could go where he wanted.

The pony's ears pricked up, and he lifted his head to sniff at the frosty air. Then he let out his breath in a puff of white and began to move forward purposefully, heading for the edge of the field. Emma could see huge heaps of snow piled up against the hedge there.

'Whoa, Sheltie! Let me listen,' said Emma. 'I thought I heard something.'

Sheltie stood very still. There wasn't the tiniest jingle from his harness.

Emma heard the noise properly this time. It was a voice. Someone was calling.

Chapter Four

'Come on, boy,' said Emma excitedly. 'Let's go and see.'

Sheltie galloped across the white field as fast as he could, leaving a trail of hoof prints behind him. As soon as they reached the bank of snow, Emma dismounted. 'Hello?' she called. 'Is anyone there?'

'Th – thank goodness,' said a shaking voice.

Emma and Sheltie walked over to where the voice was coming from.

'Are you Rosie's dad?' she called.

'Yes! I'm so glad someone's come,' continued the man. 'I thought I was going to freeze to death. I've piled snow round me to keep warm, but it's not *that* warm!'

Rosie's dad had built a wall of snow around him. Emma peered into the top. He was crouching in his little igloo. He had blue eyes and brown curly hair, just like Rosie.

'We've been looking everywhere for you,' said Emma. 'You must have gone the wrong way.'

'Yes,' said Rosie's dad. 'I'm obviously not very good at finding my way in the snow – or at building igloos! But who are you, and how do you know about Rosie? Is she all right?'

'I live near Mr Crock,' explained Emma. 'He and Rosie are looking for you too, with Mr Brown. He's got a Land Rover. If I can borrow your phone I can call him and tell him where you are,' said Emma.

'The battery ran out soon after I phoned Mr Crock,' said Rosie's dad. 'Can you help me get out of here? I'm so cold I can hardly move and I think I may have twisted my ankle.'

'Sheltie can help,' said Emma proudly. And before Rosie's dad could ask who Sheltie was, he saw the little Shetland pony's hairy face peering down at him.

'All right, boy, but be careful,' said Emma.

Sheltie pawed at the white wall with
his hoofs, and broke down the packed
snow so that it fell to the ground in
lumps.

'We're nearly there – you'll soon be
out.' She scrabbled at the snow with her
gloved hands, pulling chunks of it away.

Sheltie puffed a breath of hot air down
into the middle of the igloo, and Rosie's
dad laughed. 'Well done, Sheltie. That's

just what I needed to defrost my eyebrows!'

Emma was getting anxious. How would Rosie's dad manage to walk through the snow with a twisted ankle?

Suddenly Sheltie stopped, pricked up his ears and whinnied loudly.

'Come on, Sheltie! We've got to get Rosie's dad out before it's dark and somehow we've got to get him back to the Land Rover!' said Emma frantically.

But then she heard a call from across the snow-covered meadow. She straightened up, feeling almost as stiff as Rosie's dad.

It was Mr Brown with Rosie on his shoulders, striding over the field. Close behind came PC Green.

'He's over here!' cried Emma, feeling

relieved. 'But he's hurt his ankle.' Sheltie gave another noisy whinny of welcome and Rosie's dad let out a faint cheer.

'Daddy, Daddy!' shouted Rosie excitedly.

Mr Brown let Rosie down gently in the snow and he and PC Green hurried over to help her dad.

'It's Daddy dressed as Santa!' said Rosie.

As the two men pulled Rosie's dad out of the snow, they all saw what he was wearing. A bright red robe with white trimmings.

He had been all dressed up as Father Christmas to surprise Rosie when he arrived on Christmas Day!

Rosie's dad tried to move, but his ankle was too painful to walk across the

snowy field back to the Land Rover
where Mr Crock was waiting for them.

Emma and Rosie had an idea at
exactly the same time.

'He can ride Sheltie!' they said
together.

Mr Brown and PC Green helped
Rosie's dad on to Sheltie's back, and
tucked Rosie in front of him, wrapped

up in the red robe. Rosie's dad looked very funny with his long legs dangling down from Sheltie's broad back! His feet slid gently along the ground over the snow.

Sheltie went slowly and carefully across the field. Emma was so proud of her pony. He might be small, but Sheltie was the best rescue pony in the whole world!

Home at last, Rosie's dad thawed out in front of Mr Crock's roaring log fire, and rested his leg.

'That's the cleverest Shetland pony I've ever seen,' said Rosie's dad as he told Emma's dad how he had been found.

Emma beamed with pride. Of course,

she knew Sheltie was the cleverest pony in the whole world, but it was great when other people thought so too!

Rosie insisted on bringing Sheltie inside to give him his present of peppermints from the Christmas tree.

'Since it's a special occasion,' said Mr Crock, 'I think we could let him in.'

But cheeky Sheltie couldn't wait for his present off the Christmas tree. He looked around the room with a mischievous sparkle in his brown eyes. Then he reached out his long neck and snatched the star from the top of the tree!

'He knows he's a star!' said Rosie's dad, laughing.

Rosie and Emma looked at each other and smiled.

'He's the star I wished on,' said Rosie softly. 'And he made my wish come true!'